HIGH PLAINS CYBORG

CYBORGS OF MARS

HONEY PHILLIPS

Copyright © 2019 by Honey Phillips

All rights reserved. No part of this book may be used or reproduced by any means, graphic, electronic, or mechanical, including photocopying, recording, taping or by any information storage retrieval system without the written permission of the author.

Disclaimer

This book is a work of fiction. Names, characters, places, and incidents are products of the author's imagination or are used fictitiously and are not to be construed as real. Any resemblance to actual events, locales, organizations, or people, living or dead, is entirely coincidental.

Cover Design by Pro Book Covers Studio
Edited by Nikki Groom @ Indie Hub Editing Services

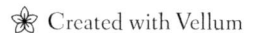

❊ Created with Vellum

ONE

C-487 stared at the ceiling of his bunk—the same bunk that had been his residence since Earth Government had sent him and his fellow cyborgs to terraform Mars, more than ten years ago. He didn't need the sleep, but now that he was amongst humans again, he tried to follow the established customs of human behavior. First there had been the scientists, moving into the labs that he and his brethren had built. Then, as soon as they had enclosed the first set of buildings that would form a town, the power plant workers came. Most of them were only in New Arcadia briefly before shipping out to one of the huge edifices that were steadily converting the polar ice into carbon dioxide, water and oxygen. He had worked on building those as well.

The miners had been next, accompanied by entrepreneurs determined to cash in on the rapidly expanding growth of the new Martian colony. And now, the first shipload of settlers, who had arrived a week ago. Today the Claims Office would allow them to start filing for their plots—the ones they would have to live on and work for the next five years in order to claim ownership of their land. If he had been in charge, he would simply have assigned each settler to a plot of land, but Earth Government had decided that each settler could choose for themselves. For the past week, the rovers had been darting around the landscape as the settlers explored the surroundings. He'd had to rescue no less than five different idiots who had overestimated either their skills or the ability of the small vehicles.

With the amount of land available for settlement, today should go smoothly, but somehow, he suspected that it would not. There had been two fights last night in one of the bars that populated the main commerce strip over which piece of rocky desert was better than another piece.

If he had still been fully human, he would have sighed. Instead, he simply gave up the attempt to mimic human behavior and rose to his feet. He pulled on the faded black pants and shirt that he had been given as part of his job and, after a moment's thought, buckled on his gun. He didn't need it—he was more than capable of taking down a few humans—but he found they respected the sight of the weapon. He fastened the gold star, a ridiculous affectation marking his position, to his chest. His hand lingered over the dark glasses but in the end, he put them on. They didn't entirely conceal his cybernetic eyes, but they did soften the effect. With his hat pulled low over his forehead, he could almost have passed for human—a very large, muscular human.

Shrugging off the notion, he exited his room and walked down a corridor lined with identical doors to the window overlooking New Arcadia. He had been a teenager when the government first began building the Green Magnetic Dipole Shield—the one that would protect Mars from solar winds and radiation and allow the planet to be terraformed. But even working two jobs, trying to make enough to support himself and his sister, he still remembered the propaganda pictures that had been everywhere. He would catch a glimpse of them walking home from the factory, his legs so tired they trembled, and would long to travel to Mars, to escape his bleak present and his hopeless future. In the pictures, everything had been white and shiny and new with gleaming metal walls and huge windows.

Now, he looked out on the reality of a frontier town. Beneath the domes enclosing New Arcadia, cheap prefab panels and recycled parts from earlier missions made up the ever-expanding business district, along with a number of structures built from regolith, the Martian dirt compressed into building material. Everything was covered with the pervasive orange dust. Not the future he had envisioned and one for which he had paid far too high a cost.

"Could be trouble." A low voice interrupted his thoughts as M-231 joined him at the window. The older model cyborg was even less visibly human than C-487, a deliberate choice by the military to make sure that no one ever forgot that they were no longer simply men.

"Trouble?"

M-231 nodded at the long line of settlers extending from the door of the Claims Office down the long central thoroughfare. Most of them were huddled against the buildings but he saw several of them already arguing, their faces flushed with cold and alcohol. The ones closest to the door were quieter, sure of their place in line, but even there he saw some restless movement. Except for one person.

Near the very front of the line, a small male pressed against the wall. Even with C-487's enhanced vision, all he could see between an oversized coat and a bright red knitted hat was a pair of big, dark eyes but something about the figure caught his attention. Surely the male was both too small and too young to apply for a claim. Still, that was the Claim Officer's concern, not his.

"I will go and remind them that law enforcement exists on Mars, just as it does on Earth." It was, after all, his job. The only one he would ever have. As the original terraforming project reached the point where it would support human life with only minor adjustments, the cyborgs were given two alternatives—return to Earth and its constant minor wars or stay on Mars and provide law enforcement for the newly arriving settlers. He had no reason to return and even less desire to fight.

"Do you want me to accompany you?" M-231 asked.

"To handle a small crowd of humans?" In his former life, he would have been insulted.

The other male dipped his head in acknowledgement and C-487 left without any additional conversation.

The sun had not yet risen and as he emerged onto the main street, he noted that the temperature inside the enclosed town was barely above freezing. GenCon, the corporation responsible for managing Martian resources, saw no reason to spend energy on heating the town beyond the absolute minimum and he tended to agree with them. Of course, the air temperature was of no concern to him. His nanites automatically adjusted to ensure that his body would neither freeze nor burn and he had long ago stopped noticing physical sensations.

As he started to head down the line to where the sound of arguing had escalated, the first ray of sunlight hit the edge of the dome, followed by the chime of the opening bell from the Claims Office. An explosion of yells erupted from the front of the line and he saw a group of men racing from where they had been concealed in a nearby alley, heading for the door to the Claims Office. The line started to dissolve into chaos as the rest of the waiting men rushed forward. His enhanced hearing picked up a soft cry and he saw a bright red hat shoved against the wall as the small male was pushed aside.

An unexpected surge of protectiveness surprised him, and he pushed his way into the fray, shoving aside struggling bodies with little thought other than to reach the figure in the red hat before he disappeared beneath the crowd.

As the Martian sky began to lighten, Jo moved away from where she had been huddled protectively against the wall. The line behind her was growing increasingly restless and she didn't trust anyone not to try and steal her place. She was fifth in line, hopefully a position which would allow her to claim the plot she had set her heart on.

It had been a long cold night, but it would be worth it to get plot 1080-3B. After a quick look at the line behind her, she moved further into the street, trying to make herself look as bulky as possible. The inexpensive thermal coat helped. Unlike the sleeker, more expensive coats, hers was stuffed with artificial fibers and added a good twenty pounds to her small frame. Unfortunately, there was nothing she could do about her lack of inches. All of the men in front of her were at least a head taller, as were most of the men behind her. She hadn't seen another woman.

Although Earth Government had done everything in their power to encourage women to apply for the Homestead program, very few had taken them up on the opportunity. She had only seen two other females on the ship—a tall, thin woman who was always at her husband's side, and an attractive curvy blonde who had half the men on the ship chasing after her. The limited number of women had not seemed to matter as much when her partner—her former partner—Nicky had been by her side.

Her mouth twisted as the familiar combination of rage and sorrow swept over her. She had known Nicky since they were both children in the orphanage and even though she had seen how often over the years he had used his charm and quick wit to duck out of his responsibilities, she hadn't expected that he would betray her so quickly. Of course, as usual he had tried to sweet talk her into thinking that his plan was a better option.

"Don't you see, Jo?" He had beamed at her from the other side of their tiny room in the transit hotel, his blue eyes sparkling. It was only their second day on Mars, and she was still trying to adjust to land that did not move. "This will be so much better. I can spend a year or two working in the power plants making a real salary, right now, instead of hoping that the claim will turn a profit in what? Three years? Four?"

"And what am I going to do, Nicky?" The power plants did not accept female employees yet.

"You can get a job here in town," he urged. "That way both of us are working and bringing in money."

She could only stare at him in dismay. So far, the few females in town who were not part of the Homestead program were either working in the whorehouse or serving drinks at one of the many bars. And she suspected that the servers were only slightly more discreet about their true source of income. Even assuming that she could evade a fate that she had been running from her entire life, a small room above a bar and evenings spent dealing with drunken men were not what she had envisioned when she had agreed to the whole idea.

"I don't want a job in town. I want to file for a claim. I want to own some land, to have a place that is actually mine. You know that, Nicky. You been listening to me talk about it since we were children."

He frowned petulantly, his eyes shifting away from her.

"We could still have that. But with the kind of money that

I'll be making at the power plant, we could just out-and-out buy a place in a year or two. We could even hire people to do the work. And we could leave it whenever we wanted."

"Leave it to go where? This is the only town in the northern district, and you know they told us that it could be years before they invest in any other towns."

He waved his hand dismissively. "I'm sure it won't be that long. And this town is expanding all the time. Wouldn't it be fun to be here watching it grow?"

The gap between them only seemed to increase in size. She didn't want to watch the town grow. She had spent her whole life trying to cling to things, even as they slipped through her fingers. The one thing she wanted more than anything else was a permanent home and she was willing to work her fingers to the bone to get that, to know that she was the one who decided if things would change and how they would change.

"That's not what we talked about, Nicky. It's not even what we agreed to when we signed the papers. Are you even sure that you can change your mind now?"

"Sure," he said quickly, but he still didn't look at her directly.

Her heart sank. She had seen that expression one too many times in the past. What a fool she had been to think that he would ever really change. When he had come to her with the wild proposition that they apply to the Homestead program, she had been too excited by the prospect to remember the number of times he had let her down in the past. Thank God she had insisted that their partnership be purely platonic. He had broken her heart at sixteen when he took her virginity and then disappeared a week later. He'd done it again at eighteen when he'd left her to be picked up by the police while he left town. At least at twenty-two she was older, and she had thought wiser. But she suspected that this betrayal would be infinitely harder to recover from than the previous two.

"I'm going to go ahead with it," she said slowly.

"Applying for a claim?"

"Yes. There was nothing in the regulations that said a single person could not apply." She shrugged, trying to appear nonchalant, even though her heart was pounding with a combination of dread and excitement. "It will be a smaller plot but that's probably just as well. It will be easier for me to manage."

His eyes turned speculative before he nodded approvingly.

"That might even be better. And no need to apply by yourself. You can just register in both our names. That way there will be no question about why I came."

"Both our names? You mean you've reconsidered?"

"No, no." He waved his hand again. "You can apply for double claim and start the homestead while I go to the power plants."

For a moment, she was actually tempted. It would allow her to get more land and perhaps once the homestead was up and running, Nicky might choose to come and live with her. But her good sense won out.

She shook her head. "No, Nicky, I won't do that. You know one of the requirements is that you have to live there full-time and you won't be there."

"I doubt that anyone is really going to check. And if they do, you can just tell them that I went into town for a few days. Right, Josie bear?"

He gave her his charming grin, blue eyes sparkling.

"I won't lie for you again, Nicky." The last time she had almost ended up in jail and the memory of the inquisition at the police station still gave her nightmares.

"Fine, then. You figure out how you going to put up a

shelter and get the power working and spread all those stupid plants."

As part of the claim agreement, she had to cover fifty percent of her land with the specially bred lichen that were designed to absorb heat from the sun and to release oxygen into the air. But she had spent most of the ninety-day voyage going over the instruction manuals provided by the government. It wouldn't be quick or easy, but it was nothing that she couldn't handle. All it would take was hard work and she'd had a lifetime of that.

"That's what I have to do, then that's what I'll do."

"Just don't come crying to me in six months when one of the dust storms destroys your shelter and rips up all your plants."

He didn't even seem to realize that in such a catastrophe she would most probably be dead. Instead, he slammed out of the room and she hadn't seen him since.

The next morning, after lingering a few extra hours just in case he had changed his mind, she set out on her search. Most of the other settlers were scoping out the plots close to town, choosing convenience as their primary goal. A few of them seemed to be banding together to stakeout a large flat area further out on the plains. She had no real interest in being close to town or in close proximity to her neighbors and each day she went further out.

On the fourth day, just as she had given up hope, she found the perfect plot. The northern side backed onto a low ridge which would provide shelter behind her while allowing a wide southern expanse to gather solar energy. The rest of it consisted of small rocky hills which could be used for both lichen and one day, the goats that were being bred especially for Mars.

Now she was determined to get that plot. She snuck a glance at the four men in front of her. She thought she recognized the first two from the ship and she knew they intended to farm. They would not be interested in her claim.

The two men directly in front of her did not look like any of the settlers. They were big beefy men wearing the coveralls of power plant workers. She hadn't realized that they too could apply for a claim.

The opening chime sounded, and the world exploded into confusion. The two men in front of her spread out their arms, blocking the sidewalk as they yelled across the street. A group of men, all big and rough-looking, poured out of an alley heading for her position. The people in line behind her, seeing the confusion at the front of the line, started to rush forward. She tried her best to hold her position, but she was no match for the onslaught of men pushing and shoving. An elbow caught her in the side, slamming her back against the wall and knocking her head hard enough that she saw stars. She swayed as her head spun and clutched the side of the building desperately. It was no longer just a question of her claim. If she went down amongst all these men, she wasn't sure she would ever make it back to her feet.

TWO

Another elbow caught Jo in the ribs, knocking her off balance, and to her horror she began to slip. Just as her knee crumpled, a strong hand gripped her elbow and hauled her upright.

Nicky? Had he come back after all? But even as the thought raced through her mind, she knew he had not been the one to catch her. His hands had never been that strong, his grip that firm. She turned to thank her rescuer but all she could see was broad shoulders and a massive back clad in a worn black shirt. He wasn't even wearing a coat and she shivered at the thought, even though the hand still grasping her elbow seemed to be radiating heat through her worn garment.

"Stay here," a low deep voice rumbled, sending a not unpleasant shiver through her body.

He stepped forward and even though she had been surrounded by a crowd of men only moments before, suddenly she had breathing room. He grabbed the two men who had been in front of her and knocked their heads together with casual, brutal ease. Both men collapsed to the ground. Another pair of men went flying, then another, and within minutes, the riot had subsided. At least twenty men were lying bleeding and bruised on the ground and silence had descended over the crowd.

Her rescuer turned back in her direction and she couldn't hide her expression of shock. He looked even bigger from this side, the seams of his shirt straining across a broad chest and his worn black pants clinging to immense thighs. All she could see of his face was a strong jaw, a straight nose, and a firm mouth, but that was not the source of her surprise. Behind heavy dark glasses, she caught a gleam of red. No man had eyes like that.

He opened his mouth to speak and light caught the tarnished gold star on his chest. Fuck. A Ranger. His strength and his ability to handle the rioting men suddenly made sense. They had been advised on the trip that the cyborgs Earth Government had utilized in the initial phases of the settlement were still on the planet. They had been granted legal powers and served as the main source of law and order. The briefing had also been quite clear that they were dangerous and should be avoided unless absolutely necessary.

She thought she saw something flicker across his face as he took in her expression, but she decided she must have been mistaken. Everyone knew cyborgs were no better than robots, all human emotions removed during the process that turned them into what they were—workers, weapons, machines to be used as the government saw fit.

Something that felt almost like pain flickered through C-487 at the familiar horror on the face of the small male but he dismissed the notion. Pain was not an emotion; pain was lying on a lab table while a group of scientists discussed which parts of his body were worth saving. Pain was hearing that his eyes no longer functioned. Pain was feeling the nanites invading his bloodstream, turning him from a man into a machine.

Making a note to run diagnostics later, he turned to the crowd of subdued settlers. All of the men who had attempted to jump the line were sprawled on the ground around him and he took a quick survey. Injured but not dead. He paid no further attention to them.

"You may proceed to register. No more than five people at a time within the office." He looked down the line. Very few of them dared to meet his eyes. "Do not attempt to modify your place in line. I do not like line-jumpers." He gestured at the nearby bodies.

To his surprise, he caught a small startled laugh from the male he had rescued. He was still not quite sure what had driven him to protect the youngster, but he told himself that he simply did not want to deal with another body.

The boy pulled his hat further down over his ears, then straightened his shoulders and got back into position behind the first two settlers. C-487 saw him wince as he moved and once again an unexpected flare of something that felt a lot like anger went through him.

He had always felt driven to protect those weaker than himself. It was one of the things that had driven him to join the military after his sister died. That and the fact that it was one of the few jobs on Earth with a guarantee that one would be fed, clothed, and housed. Unfortunately, he had not realized that the price would be so high.

The door to the Claims Office opened and Smith poked out a cautious head.

"All clear?"

All of the travelers to Mars had to pass a fitness test and he couldn't help but wonder how exactly Smith had managed to pass the test. A tall, thin man with a balding head, he didn't look capable of doing more than lifting his paperwork.

"Yes. You may begin," he ordered.

The first five settlers shuffled forward, including the boy, and although he had intended to stay outside and keep an eye on the crowd, he found himself following him into the small office.

Smith shivered and hurried back behind his desk, turning up the heat in an already overheated room. C-487 automatically adjusted his body temperature but he noticed that the settlers looked uncomfortably warm. All of them except his little male took off their outer garments. The boy remained huddled in his cheap thermal coat, even though C-487 could see strip of face between his hat and collar turning pink.

"Remove your garments before you faint," he ordered, striding over to the small figure and pulling off his hat. Fuck. *Her* hat. He looked down into a pair of indignant brown eyes and an emotion he thought had been drilled out of him many years ago suddenly resurfaced. *Mine.*

JO STARED UP AT THE CYBORG IN BAFFLED AMAZEMENT. Why was he being so bossy? And why would he care about whether or not she was too hot? She had to admit that removing the hat had helped. A blush rose to her cheeks despite the heat already infusing them with color. All of the other men were staring at her too. Her cyborg made a growling noise and stepped in front of her, then removed his own hat. After a brief pause, the other men followed suit.

"Um, can we get started?" the weedy looking man behind the desk asked, with a nervous look at the cyborg.

"Proceed."

One of the first two settlers looked at her, then at the Ranger. "Would you like to go first?"

"No! I mean, you were here first."

He hesitated, then nodded and turned to the clerk, reeling out the coordinate for his chosen parcel. Nowhere near hers, thank goodness. The clerk nodded, registered the claim, then issued a ticket to be exchanged for the initial set of equipment provided by the government. She knew a few of the passengers on the ship planned to purchase additional materials, but she had no extra money and the government supplies were all she would have to live on.

The second settler's plot was also in another sector. Finally, it was her turn and she stepped up to the desk.

"Plot 1080-3B, please."

The man drew it up on the map, then gave her a worried look. "Are you sure? This is at least a two-hour drive from New Arcadia, and I don't expect to see a lot of interest in that area."

"That's fine."

It was, in fact, one of the things that had attracted her to the land. No close neighbors meant little chance for trouble. Although no one had made an advance on her, now that Nicky had left, she was extremely conscious of the fact that she was a lone female amongst a number of males.

The clerk shook his head but began filling out the records. "I assume this is for a double claim? What is the other name?"

For a moment, she was almost tempted to give him Nicky's name. The extra land would be nice, and it might even help him out if the officials discovered he had abandoned the Homestead program for the power plants. But she refused to take the chance of having everything taken from her if the deception was uncovered.

"Just one plot. In my name."

"Who will protect you?"

The deep voice startled her, and she jumped. Her cyborg was standing next to her, frowning down with that intimidating red glare. And yet, she didn't feel threatened. She had the oddest urge to smooth away his frown.

"I'm quite capable of protecting myself."

She pulled back the side of her coat to reveal the holster of her gun. He stared at the gap in her clothing and a rush of heat swept over her when she realized that he was studying her body rather than the weapon. She quickly pulled her coat closed and watched as he finally dragged his gaze away.

"Do you know how to use that?"

"Of course. I've had over a hundred hours of training." All of it on the ship's virtual range, of course, but he didn't need to know that.

For a second she thought he was about to speak, but he merely inclined his head and stepped back. The rest of the registration was completed quickly, and the clerk handed her the documents she would need to pick up her supplies.

"You can get them any time in the next five days, but I wouldn't wait too long," he said with a wry smile. "Things have been known to go missing."

"I won't wait," she promised. "I'll go this morning."

"I will escort you," the cyborg said.

"You don't need to do that." She raised her chin. "I know where the supply depot is located. And besides, don't you need to stay here and watch over the crowd?"

He hesitated for a fraction of a second, then gave a curt nod and strode out of the Claims Office.

She stared after the departing cyborg, resisting a sudden urge to call him back.

You don't need him, she reminded herself. *It only makes you weak when you start depending on others.* Firming her chin, she pulled her hat down over her head again, buttoned her coat, and started off in the direction of the supply depot.

The large building at the edge of the town appeared to be deserted. Apparently, the other settlers weren't quite as ready to leave. Following the instructions on the sign, she punched her name into the computer terminal, then paced impatiently, too restless to take a seat in the small waiting area.

"Jo Taylor," the supply master called, and she stepped forward eagerly.

A stocky older man with a grizzled face, he looked from his list to her face, then back again. "Jo Taylor?" he repeated doubtfully.

"Yes, that's me."

"Is this a mistake? It says here you have registered for a single claim."

"That's right."

He gave her another doubtful look, then shook his head. "Reckon you know what you're doing." He led her over to one side of the big warehouse. "This is your personal rover. You stick it out for five years and it's yours to keep. Make sure you keep the bearings free of sand and it will last that long without any problem. The sled contains all of the supplies promised in the brochure. You did study the brochure, right?"

"Of course, I did." She walked around the packed sled, pointing out the various packages. "This is the shelter and the solar panels. The hydroponic system is in there, plus the lichen spores. Air mattress and furnishings, initial food supplies, and the Radioisotope Thermoelectric Generator for heating and power."

"Don't forget. You gotta start—"

"—the hydroponic garden right away. I know the food supplies aren't intended to last more than a few months."

He laughed. "Reckon you'll do, girlie. Want me to hold this for you while you say your goodbyes?"

"No need," she said as cheerfully as possible. "I'm ready to go."

She had already picked up the small bag containing all of her worldly possessions. Reaching into it, she grabbed the small nose mask that provided supplemental oxygen and pushed it into place. The initial terraforming efforts had raised the atmospheric pressure to the point where suits were no longer required, but humans still required supplemental oxygen. She had read that the cyborgs didn't require them and for a moment her mind flashed back to that tall, broad figure.

"Airlock over there," the supply master said, recalling her mind to the present. He pointed to the rear of the building, then offered her his hand. "Good luck, girlie."

Startled but unexpectedly touched, she gave him a shaky smile and shook his hand. "Thank you."

She maneuvered her way through the airlock and onto the rocky surface feeling unexpectedly buoyant. The feeling lasted the entire trip and it wasn't until she reached her new home, that the impact of what she was taking on really sank in. She pulled the rover to a stop in front of the rocky ledge she had chosen to be the back wall of her new home and stepped out onto her land. *Her land.* Ahead of her, the landscape sprawled out in a vast expanse of orange and gold desert, interspersed with strange rock outcroppings scoured by the prevailing winds, and topped by a pale orange sky. Behind her, the land rose sharply into a craggy mountain range. To others it might have looked lonely, but after a lifetime cooped up in tiny rooms, always surrounded by people, by buildings, by the constant chaos of life on Earth, she could see the beauty and serenity in the desolate landscape.

With a smile on her face, she started to unpack the sled. By the time the pale sun was setting over the horizon, she was tired, dirty, and every muscle of her body ached. It was a good thing that Mars' gravity was so much lower than Earth's she thought with a grimace. Even though she had studied the instructions multiple times, she hadn't accounted for the amount of sheer physical labor that was required in assembling everything. But that only added to her feeling of satisfaction as she stepped back and surveyed her accomplishments.

The initial shelter was in place—an inflatable dome held in place by a framework of Martian iron. Tomorrow she would assemble the interconnected dome to house the hydroponic system. If she had been able to afford them, she would also have purchased a third dome and two of the goats they were breeding for life on Mars, but she would have to wait until she received the small government stipend at the end of her first year before expanding her holdings. In the meantime, she would make do with what she had.

With a tired sigh, she entered her airlock and removed her breathing mask. Too exhausted to do more than eat half a protein bar, she adjusted the RTG to provide enough heat to combat the freezing overnight temperatures, laid down on the mattress in the small sleeping alcove, and was asleep before the sky turned completely dark.

On a ridge overlooking the new claim, C-487 watched as the lights dimmed in the small shelter. As soon as the majority of the settlers had registered their claims, he had headed for his horse. Not the actual animals but rather mechanical simulations, horses were faster than the rovers and made it easier to travel over a wide variety of terrain. He had reached her claim by mid-afternoon and it had taken all of his will power not to go down and assist her as she struggled through the assembly of her dwelling. She had made it clear that she wanted to proceed on her own and he would allow her that—for now.

But even as he turned his horse back to town, he was already thinking of ways in which he could assist her. She was his to protect and this time, he would not fall down on that duty.

THREE

It was the quiet that woke Jo from a confused dream involving the cyborg and an absence of clothing. On Earth there was a constant buzz of noise from too many people living too close to each other. On the ship, it had been the constant hum of the engines along with more people crammed into a small space. And even after they arrived in New Arcadia, there had been the other settlers in the transient hotel, along with the noises of the town itself. But now she was alone, the only person for miles around, and outside of her shelter nothing disturbed the surrounding desert. The silence was both peaceful and slightly nerve-wracking, but this was her life now and she would just have to get used to it.

The weak Martian sunlight was already setting the transparent portions of her shelter aglow. Time to get to work. She had stripped down to a tank and panties for sleeping and she grimaced as she went to pull on her dusty outdoor clothing. Getting the water drill working was next on her list. As soon as that was working, she would have access to water for drinking and bathing and she could set up the shelter for her hydroponic garden. After a quick protein bar and a few sips from one of her precious bottles of water, she donned her coat and mask and headed outside.

As she began unpacking the supplies for the drill and the second shelter, she took a moment to look out over her land, appreciating the subtle colors as the sunlight began to illuminate the rocky ground. Scanning the horizon, she saw a lone figure on top of a rocky outcrop—one that looked for all the world like a cowboy astride a horse. A horse, here?

She blinked and shook her head. When she looked back, the figure was gone. She must have been imagining it, based on her dream about the cyborg. Would she ever see him again, she wondered? She knew that some of the Rangers were assigned to patrol the territory surrounding New Arcadia—maybe he would come out to check on her. Her pulse fluttered at the idea before she firmly pushed it aside. She was here to make a home for herself, not to get lost in lustful dreams about someone who was more machine than man.

Assembling the water drill turned out to be more complicated than she had anticipated but she forced herself to read each instruction twice and finally succeeded in putting it together. She gave it a satisfied look before turning to decide on the best location for the device. Once it was in place, it would drill down through the soil until it reached the ice pack underlying much of the Martian soil. From there, it would convert the ice into water and pump it back up for her to use.

Eventually she decided that the side of the ridge closest to her shelter would be most convenient and began moving it into position, once again grateful for the low gravity that allowed her to move the heavy device.

"You don't want it there."

A startled yell escaped her lips as she spun to face the owner of the voice, her hand going instinctively to her gun belt

—or where her gun belt would have been if she had remembered to put it on that morning. Her cyborg cowboy stood there, frowning as he followed her movement.

"Where is your weapon?"

"I... I didn't think it was necessary," she said defiantly. "I wasn't expecting visitors."

"Which is precisely why you should be wearing it," he pointed out. "You should be armed at all times."

"You mean in case someone decides to sneak up on me?"

"I did not sneak. I rode in."

He nodded at his horse, except it wasn't an actual horse. Rather a collection of rusted-looking metal pieces was assembled into a robotic representation of the animal. She had never seen one of the increasingly rare beasts on Earth of course, but she had always loved old books about horses. It stood patiently behind him, and she could have sworn that its eyes studied her face.

"I didn't know these existed on Mars," she said. "Can I touch it?"

"It is just metal," he said dismissively.

"Not just metal," she said, running her hand down a mane of small flexible tubes. The robot seemed to shift into her touch, and she laughed with delight. "What's his name?"

"It does not have a name. It is a machine."

"He needs a name. I think... I think Red Beauty."

He snorted. "Red, perhaps, but not Beauty." He studied her face. "You consider him, *it* beautiful?"

"Well, of course." The realization clicked into place. "Were you watching me this morning? From that ridge?"

As soon as she spoke, an embarrassed heat rose to her cheeks. Of course, he wouldn't have been watching her. She must have just seen him on his rounds.

"Yes," he said, interrupting her tumbled thoughts.

"You were? Why?"

"I wished to make sure you were safe."

Huh. Despite a pleasant little tingle that she refused to acknowledge, she frowned at him. "Why did you think I might need help? Because I'm female?"

"Yes." He gave her a long, slow look that made her nipples ache and caused a sudden rush of heat between her legs.

"There are other female settlers," she pointed out. "Are you going to watch over them as well?"

"I am not interested in them."

More heat rose to her cheeks. He was interested in her? But…

"I didn't think cyborgs were interested in women," she blurted out.

Something flashed across his face, interrupting his normal emotionless expression.

"It is not encouraged." Before she could open her mouth to respond, he turned back to the water drill. "You do not want to locate the machine here."

"Why not? It registered the presence of subsurface ice. I thought it would be close to the shelter and the ridge would help protect it from dust storms." The thought made her shiver. They had been warned over and over about the danger of the inevitable dust storms.

"The ice is much further beneath the ground in this location." He lifted the heavy water drill with one hand—*one hand* —and carried it easily to a new location further along the ridge. "This will still provide some protection, but the ice is closer to the surface, and you will have better exposure for the solar array."

He began to run through the initial setup process, then stopped and turned to her. "Is this acceptable?"

She had been jockeying between annoyance at the way he

had taken over and gratitude that he had saved her from making a mistake, but his question, and the slightly anxious way he asked it, swung her over into gratitude.

"Yes, that would be wonderful. Thank you."

He gave a curt nod, then finished the sequence to deploy the machine. As it began drilling down into the surface, she remembered the collection basket and went to grab it. The crushed rock would be used in building her garden. She placed the basket under the output and watched in satisfaction as small rocks began to clatter into it.

"How did you know?" she asked.

"Know what?"

"That the ice would be closer to the surface here?"

C-487 HESITATED, ODDLY RELUCTANT TO REVEAL THE source of his knowledge. Would reminding her of his differences make her pull away from him? He had seen a variety of emotions flash across that expressive little face since his arrival —her initial fear replaced by defiance as that pointed little chin rose, her delight in his horse, even something that looked like appreciation when she snuck a glance at him. The memory of that was enough to cause his cock to stir just as it had done then, the sensation as shocking as it had been the first time. His body did not respond unless he willed it, except with her. Once again, he forced himself under control.

Of all the expressions that had crossed her face, he had never seen anything resembling the usual mistrust with which most humans viewed cyborgs. He did not want to see it on her face now. But she had asked...

He gestured reluctantly at his eyes, still masked behind his glasses. "I have enhanced vision, including infrared. I can detect temperature differentials."

He did not mention that after realizing that he did not want to leave her, he had returned to his vantage point and spent most of the night studying her claim and identifying the features that would be most useful to her. Or that he had frequently found his gaze traveling back to the small bright glow of her body in the shelter.

"Oh. Well, that's kind of cool."

She smiled up at him and his breath—the breath he didn't need to survive—caught in his chest. He had never seen a more beautiful sight. He took a half-step towards her before he came to his senses.

"What do you intend to do next?" he asked gruffly.

"I need to set up the dome for the hydroponic garden and attach it to the shelter." She looked confused at his brusqueness and he had to fight down the urge to pull her into his arms and smooth the frown from her brow.

"I will assist." Before she could protest, he turned and headed for the sled, determined to bury these new and unexpected emotions in work.

By the time the sun dropped close to the horizon, the water drill had begun to produce a slow but steady stream of icy water. Jo had used the insulated pipeline to connect it to her greenhouse, now fully assembled and waiting for the next step— building the array of tanks and planters where she would hopefully be able to produce her food supply. The day had gone more quickly and efficiently that she had expected, thanks to her cyborg cowboy. If not for him, she would have been much further behind.

But more than his assistance, she was grateful for his presence. For the presence of another living being in the desolate landscape. The thought brought her to a sudden halt. Not even one full day on her own and she was already grateful for company. Company that was not going to stay. What was she doing? Hadn't her experiences with Nicky taught her that she couldn't rely on anyone but herself?

She looked over at her cyborg. He was checking the connections on the water line and as if he felt her watching him, he looked up. Her eyes met his, the red glow behind the dark glasses already familiar to her, and her heart gave a little skip.

This is ridiculous, she told herself firmly. *He's just being nice. It doesn't mean you can start depending on him.*

While she was lecturing herself, he finished his inspection and came over to her. For a big man, he moved with surprising silence and grace.

"Thank you for helping me today," she said, trying to sound appropriately formal. "I'm sure you must have other more important matters to attend to."

"No."

"Oh. Well, I don't want to keep you." She cringed inside at how rude that sounded.

One of those rare hints of emotion crossed his face. Was it hurt? Surely not.

"Are you asking me to leave?" he said bluntly.

"It's just... I appreciate the help, but I need to know how to do all these things for myself. I know it might take a little longer but you're not always going to be around."

His body went still. Then with a curt nod, he turned and headed for Red. The robotic animal had been wandering around quietly all day, adding to the illusion that it was a real animal, even though he had assured her it was just seeking out micronutrients in the soil.

Even his back looked stiff, his stride no longer so graceful, and she felt a wave of embarrassment. She had to let him go but she didn't have to be rude about it, after all.

"Wait a minute," she called, and he stopped immediately, turning back to face her. "You never told me your name."

"I am called C-487," he said slowly.

"That's not a name. Don't you have a human name?"

If anything, he stiffened even further. "I am not human."

"You were," she said indignantly. "And part of you still is, isn't it?"

He shrugged but his face didn't match the casual gesture. "Perhaps."

"What were you called? Before?"

There was a long pause and she was afraid he wouldn't answer her.

"Clint. My name was Clint," he said finally.

"It's nice to meet you, Clint. I'm Jo."

"Yes, you said that before. But that's not your full name, is it?"

She blushed. "No. It's really Josephine. But that's such an old-fashioned name."

"It is a beautiful name and it suits you." For the briefest second, his hand cupped her chin, raising her face to his, and leaving a trail of warmth behind. "Goodnight, Josephine."

He turned and mounted the horse and rode off without looking back. She raised her hand to her face, pressing her fingers to the skin he had caressed so briefly, and watched until he disappeared into the sunset. Then she hurried into her shelter, determined to begin her new life alone.

FOUR

Once again, the quiet woke Jo from a convoluted dream involving her cyborg. Her nipples throbbed beneath her thin tank and she could feel the damp heat between her thighs. What was it about him that triggered her arousal to such an extent? Yes, he was big, but there had been plenty of big men on the settlement ship. The kind of man who applied for a claim on a risky new planet did not tend to be small. Was it his air of utter confidence? The knowledge that he would be able to handle anything that came his way? No, she didn't think it was that, either. Nicky had that same air of confidence—although with considerably less reason.

Shaking her head, she pushed the useless speculation aside. After the way she had sent him off the previous day, she doubted that she would see him again. Ignoring the desolation that thought caused, she took her first quick shower in her new home and resolutely avoided thinking of Clint. She had no time to waste on mysterious strangers. There was work to be done.

Throughout the long, hard day setting up the equipment

for her garden, she found her gaze frequently straying towards the east ridge, but she never saw a tall figure on a mechanical horse. Still, she did not let that deter her from finishing the next item on her list. By the time the sun set, the grow tanks had been assembled and the nutrient solution mixed with the water. She would leave the door between the two habitats open tonight so she could hear the soft drip of the circulating water. Tomorrow she would plant.

It had been a productive day and she was actually a little further along than she had expected to be—mainly because of Clint's help the previous day. Tonight, she was not as tired and after one of the nutritious but tasteless MREs, she sat crossed legged on her mattress and stared out into the night. Not a light to be seen anywhere except that of the stars and the thin strips of ice clouds as they floated high in the sky.

The landscape was even more beautiful at night, the harsh desert concealed in the darkness, leaving only the striking contours of the rocks silhouetted against the sky. She could see a distant haze, far across the valley, no doubt one of the atmosphere-producing power plants releasing gases into the air. Was Nicky working there? Perhaps it was just as well that he had not decided to join her. She couldn't picture him living here in the silent isolation. Firmly suppressing the thought that she could easily imagine Clint sitting next to her and staring out into the night, she turned off her small light and crawled into bed.

C-487 WATCHED AS THE SHELTER DIMMED, SWITCHING TO infrared once more so that he could still see the patch of heat that her body produced. He had spent the day watching her but this time he had chosen a more isolated position. Every time she had staggered as she transported a heavy load from the sled to the shelter, he'd had to force himself not to go to her assistance. She had made it clear that she wanted to set up her home by herself and he respected her desires. To a certain extent. He would not let her overwork herself or become ill. And from what he had seen, she had only the most basic equipment issued by Earth Government, with none of the small luxuries that many of the settlers had brought with them or paid extra to acquire. He ached to make her more comfortable, but he suspected that she would reject any outright gift. Of course, if he could arrange for her to think that she was doing him a favor...

He took one last look around the valley, searching for any signs of life but all was still. No other heat signatures were present. She would be safe if he left her long enough to return to town.

"Come on, Big Red," he said to his horse, and set a fast pace back to New Arcadia. He would be back before she woke.

ONCE AGAIN, JO WOKE HOT AND FLUSHED, HER BODY STILL pulsing with desire for Clint. In this dream, the water pump had miraculously produced a fountain of hot water and he had tugged her beneath it, tearing off her clothes before caressing her with wet slippery hands. He followed the path of his hands with his mouth bringing her nipples to tight throbbing peaks before traveling down her body, reaching her clit just before she jolted awake.

"This is ridiculous," she muttered, but she gave into the inevitable. Her fingers snuck into her panties, finding the hard, slippery nub of her clit. She swirled her finger around it, already on the edge of climax, but the sensation danced just out of reach. It wasn't until she pictured Clint striding in through the airlock, finding her half naked and touching herself, that she exploded in a quick hard climax. Her body was still limp with satisfaction when she heard a demanding knock on the outside door of the airlock.

When she took a quick peek through the portholes, her heart skipped a beat. Clint stood outside, looking just as hard and demanding as he had been in her fantasy. He looked as though he could walk straight through both doors and into her arms. He knocked again, his usually expressionless face almost eager.

"Josephine, I know that you are in there."

He seemed to be staring straight at her and her cheeks heated at the memory of what she had been doing. Pushing aside her embarrassment, she hastily pulled on her pants, then flicked the com.

"You can come in."

Now why had she done that? Wouldn't it have been more sensible to meet him outside? But before she could reconsider, he was through the second door and standing in front of her. With an almost bashful expression, he removed his cowboy hat to reveal short dark hair that curled just a little around his ears. She had thought he was big when he was standing over her in the Claims Office, but he seemed even bigger here in her home, dominating the small space with his presence.

His nostrils flared and she saw that red gaze travel down over her body. He couldn't know what she'd been doing before he arrived. Could he?

"Uh, what are you doing here?" she said quickly, determined to ignore his strange reaction.

At her words, his gaze snapped to her face. "I need a favor."

She stared at him in surprise. How could she possibly assist him? But, of course, there was no way to refuse. In fact, she felt a pleasant little glow that she could do something to return his kindness.

"Yes, of course. What do you want me to do?"

"You don't even want to know what I am going to ask you?" A flicker of something that could have been amusement crossed that stern face.

"No. I'm happy to do anything I can to repay you."

That was definitely a scowl. "I am not asking for payment."

"I know you're not," she said quickly. "I just meant that I'm glad to have a way to show my gratitude."

The words hung in the air between them and she suddenly hoped—prayed—that he wasn't like most men and that he wouldn't make a suggestive comment about how she could demonstrate her gratitude. The lingering heat between her legs indicated that she might not find the idea totally distasteful, but she wanted more than that from him.

To her relief, he simply nodded his acceptance of her apology and reached inside his coat. She realized this was the first time she had seen him button it up. The cold never seemed to bother him. Reaching inside, he pulled out a small yellow ball of fluff, then another, and another until six little balls were curled in his big hands. She caught a glimpse of a bright black eye, then a cautious cheep.

"Chicks? You brought me chicks?"

The frozen embryos had been brought from Earth to be added to the micro environments that the settlers were creating, but they were ridiculously expensive and she had long since decided that, like the goats, she wouldn't be able to afford them until the second, or even third stipend.

"That's the favor. I need someone to raise them and take care of them until my... friend is in a position to take them."

Irresistibly drawn to the tiny creatures, she stroked a finger across one downy head. She would love to have the company but...

"I wish I could, but I can't afford the feed." She raised her chin as she spoke, refusing to feel shame for her lack of means.

"No, of course not. I wouldn't expect you to provide for them. I have a bag of feed outside. It should last until your garden starts to produce. And I would be happy to bring you more if necessary. I brought their habitat as well."

She stared at him, at a loss for words. It was an incredibly generous arrangement. She would have the comfort of their presence, their droppings to provide nutrients for her garden, and possibly even eggs if he left them with her long enough.

"I don't understand. If you have all of the equipment, why can't your friend take care of them himself?"

"He's, uh, working long hours right now."

"Extra shifts, you mean?"

He shrugged a shoulder, a remarkably human gesture. "Something like that."

"And you can't take them?" A thought struck her. "You do have a home, don't you?"

"Of a sort. But it's not equipped for livestock."

That left her without an argument. One of the tiny chicks was trying to climb out of his hands and she took it from him, brushing the soft down against her cheek.

"I'm going to call this one Columbus since he's such an explorer."

"Better make that Mrs. Columbus. They're all female. I'll get... I mean, *he'll* get a rooster later, when he has space."

The slip did not escape her notice and she gave him a suspicious look. "You do have a friend, don't you?"

"Yes." He hesitated slightly. "His name is M-231."

Of course, she should have known his only companions

would be other cyborgs. It had just never occurred to her that they might want homes of their own.

"Then I'll be happy to take care of them for him."

The chick snuggled down in her palm, warm and soft and alive, and she couldn't help her delighted grin. She was going to have company after all.

FIVE

C-487 forced himself to concentrate on assembling the habitat for the chickens, trying to ignore his throbbing, aching cock. Ever since he had walked into the shelter and caught the delicious scent of Josephine's arousal and seen the heat still radiating from between her legs, his cock had refused to obey his commands. Nothing would satisfy his body except burying himself in that sweet, hot little cunt and he was not about to risk the progress he had made today by making an advance on her.

He was well aware that human females were told to avoid cyborgs. Even the whores in the town would refuse one openly —although he knew of several that were perfectly willing to take their money when no one was looking. He had never chosen to make the attempt. He remembered only too well the damage that lifestyle had done to his mother and the price his sister had paid. *No.* He refused to think of that. Instead, he concentrated on putting together the coop.

When the habitat was completed, he helped her place the chicks inside. They rushed around making excited little cheeping noises, then settled under the heat lamp in a single fluffy pile.

"They grow rapidly," he warned her. "I will bring the materials to expand their habitat on my next trip."

"Clint." She stepped closer and put a hand on his arm. It was the first time she had touched him voluntarily and the feel of those small fingers burned through his shirt.

"Yes, Josephine?" His voice sounded distant in his own ears. It took all of his considerable self-control not to sweep her up in her arms, carry her back to her mattress, and show her how much he wanted her.

"Thank you." She looked up at him with big dark eyes. "You didn't have to bring the chicks to me to raise but I'm so glad you did."

"You're welcome. But I chose you because I know you will care for them."

"And because you knew I was lonely?"

"Are you?"

Her eyes went distant. "Yes. And no. I have spent most of my life surrounded by people and I always wanted to get away. To have a chance to be by myself."

He understood. His life had been the same until he had been chosen for the cyborg program. After that, he spent far more time alone than he had ever thought possible.

"But it isn't quite what you envisioned?"

"Yes. Do you know how I feel?"

"More than you can imagine." He thought back to those first days on Mars. The jobs they were assigned were difficult, dangerous, and frequently solitary. Earth Government had never encouraged them to associate with each other and he suspected that they had kept them apart on purpose.

"It's just so much more... desolate than I had imagined." Her eyes were still staring off into the distance. "Sometimes during the day, I look up and all I see are miles and miles of empty land. And at night, there is nothing but the stars."

"Yes. I am very familiar with both of those sights." Unable to resist, he cupped her face, delighting in the soft, smooth texture of her skin beneath his fingers.

Her hand came up to cover his, not to push him away but to press his hand more firmly against her cheek. She smiled, but he caught the hint of tears in her eyes.

"Why does it feel like you know me better than anyone I've ever met?" she asked.

"I want to know everything about you."

Giving in to temptation, he bent down and kissed her, a gentle brush of his lips against hers. She didn't respond, and he started to raise his head, but then her hands came up to circle his neck and she pulled him back down, clinging to him with fierce desperation as her mouth opened under his and her tongue tentatively brushed against his. His control disappeared. He lifted her into his arms, bringing her closer, tighter. She was all soft, warm woman in his arms, and he could feel her nipples rubbing against his chest as she squirmed closer. One of her hands sank into the short strands of his hair, tugging urgently, the other clasped his shoulder, her small nails sending a delightful prick of sensation straight to his cock. He could feel the heat of her sweet little cunt against his stomach. He had never been so close to exploding from a kiss. His hand slid up under her tank, wanting to feel more of her skin, and she shivered, then suddenly froze.

He felt the tension in her small frame and immediately lifted his head.

"Josephine?"

She wouldn't meet his eyes. "I... We shouldn't be doing this."

His long-forgotten heart ached but he very carefully set her down. As soon as he left, he was going to need to find a rock to smash his fist against. Hopefully that pain would replace this one.

"I apologize. For a moment I forgot that I am no longer a man." He turned to leave and once more her fingers closed over his arm.

"What? No, that's not what I meant."

"No?"

"No, of course not. You're very much a man." Her cheeks flamed as her eyes seemingly dropped involuntarily to his still obvious erection. "But I'm trying to do this on my own. I... I can't depend on anyone else."

"Can't or won't?" he said softly.

"Maybe a little of both? In my experience, depending on someone else only leads to disappointment."

He wanted to assure her that she could count on him, that he would never let her down, but he suspected that his words would not be sufficient. He would have to prove his worth. Patience, he told himself.

"Very well, Josephine. But there are some people you can count on."

Her mouth formed a perfect little oh, and he couldn't resist. He dropped one last, quick kiss on her sweet mouth and left before his good intentions deserted him.

Josephine stared after Clint. Had she done the right thing by sending him away? Her long-neglected body adamantly disagreed. Yet it would be far too easy to rely on his strength. She needed to know she could depend on herself.

A small cheep sounded from below and one of the chicks peeped up at her. She laughed. "You aren't worried about strength, are you?"

She picked up the small ball of fluff and cuddled it before sighing and returning the chick to her habitat. She had work to do.

Despite her conviction, her heart still lifted two days later when she looked up from spreading her lichen mixture over the rocks to see a tall figure riding towards her. He looked like an image from an old Earth movie, strong and competent and somehow at home in the desolate landscape. She remembered the way he had understood her when she spoke of the joys and terrors of loneliness. How much more must he have experienced over his years on Mars.

"Hi, Clint."

"Josephine. I brought the supplies to begin building the larger habitat for the chickens."

He spoke stiffly, his face as carved from stone as it had been the first day that she met him, and she wondered if she had offended him. That had never been her intention.

"Thank you." Before he moved away, she rushed on. "Do you want to join me for lunch? It's just MREs but I'm going to take the first cutting from the duckweed and see if it helps to improve them."

"You want me to join you?" he asked slowly.

"Yes." She knew she was blushing. "If you want to, I mean."

"I would be honored."

The stiffness left his body and his mouth twisted in what was surely a smile. Her heart lifted much more than it should have at the mere prospect of having a lunch companion, but she resolutely ignored it. She still had every intention of proving her independence, but she wouldn't hurt him by constantly pushing him away. She would just have to make sure that he understood that she could take care of herself.

Her resolve was thoroughly tested over the next month. Clint showed up every few days, almost always with some small way to make her life easier, even if it was just with his companionship. He listened to all of her plans with rapt attention, but never volunteered his opinion unless she asked—or unless she suggested something that he thought dangerous. He frequently ended up helping her as well, but as time passed and she grew more confident in her own abilities, his help no longer seemed as threatening to her ability to take care of herself.

She even managed to convince herself that her constant awareness of his big body, the warmth of his skin, the subtle scent of leather and man, were the natural result of an extended period without male companionship. But while she could be sensible during the daytime, at night she still dreamed of him, hot, hungry dreams that left her panties soaked and her body aching with desire.

SIX

"You have not been spending much time in town," M-231 observed, coming up besides Clint as he stared out over the town.

He had been automatically noting the changes—the influx of new faces, the additional buildings springing up like mushrooms—but his thoughts were far away.

"No," he agreed.

"You have been with the little female, have you not?"

He hesitated. He did not want to discuss Josephine with anyone, but it was a reasonable question.

"Yes."

"And she... accepts you? Or is she just using you to perform work for her?"

A startled laugh escaped before he could prevent it and M-231 stared at him. Humor had been drilled out of all the cyborgs a long time ago.

"I wish she would use me. It is very difficult to get her to accept any help from me." He shook his head. "My female is very stubborn."

"*Your* female?" A trace of something that looked like longing crossed M-231's face.

"Yes," he said immediately, then sighed. "At least, that is how I consider her. I am not sure that she recognizes my claim."

No matter how fervently he wished she would. She seemed to have accepted that he would show up every few days and she had been gradually accepting more of his help—especially if he could think of some way to present it as if she were doing him a favor. His last ploy had been that helping her to spread the lichen mixture would help him maintain his flexibility. The process consisted of almost continuous bending over in order to paint the substance over the rocks that cluttered the soil. She had given him a suspicious look, running her eyes over his body in a way that made his cock threaten to escape his control once more. But in the end, she had shrugged and relented, even though she still insisted on accompanying him and doing her own share of the work.

"At least you have hope."

"And you do not?" The longing in M-231's voice captured Clint's attention. "Is there a female in whom you are interested?"

M-231 moved over to the window, his robotic hand clenching on the frame. "I might have been. But she is taken. By a human."

"My female arrived with a male, but he deserted her. Perhaps..."

"No. He seems to be a good male. For a human."

There was nothing he could say, no hope he could offer. He could only imagine the pain that M-231 must be in, under the circumstances. Just the thought of Josephine being claimed by another man turned his vision red with anger. He bent his head in acknowledgement before he turned to return to his room, then paused.

"What were you called? Before..."

The other man finally turned away from the window, leaving a portion of the frame bent in the shape of his hand. "Why do you ask?"

"My Josephine. She likes to name things. My horse, her chickens. And me. She calls me by my name." He hesitated, the words unexpectedly difficult. "It is Clint."

M-231 stared at him, but just as Clint was about to give up on a response, he answered.

"Morgan. My name was Morgan."

Clint inclined his head. "Good night, Morgan."

After he returned to his room, he laid on his bunk and tried to think of a reason to return to Josephine tomorrow. He had foolishly told her that his patrol took him by her homestead every three days, but he did not want to wait another day to see her again. Would she believe him if he said it had changed to every two days? He knew she enjoyed seeing him—he saw the way her eyes lit up. He even knew that she was physically attracted to him. The scent of her arousal and the increase in her temperature were obvious. And yet, she had never acted upon the attraction. She had never even indicated that she wished to repeat their kiss, even though he had caught her watching him sometimes with a wistful look on her face.

Should he be the one to take action? His cock jerked at the thought and he sternly suppressed it. Although he longed for another taste of that tempting little mouth, of the delicious essence permanently imprinted in his memory banks, he did not want to frighten her, or even worse, have her refuse to see him. *Patience*, he reminded himself. All of the cyborgs had been programmed to take their time, to wait for the right moment, but he had never found it as hard as he did right now. Perhaps he would go spend the night on the ridge where he could watch her shelter. Knowing that she was close and that he was watching over her would be better than just lying here thinking of her. As he was sitting up, a sharp knock on the door was followed immediately by M-231—by Morgan.

"Dust storm coming. From the north. Is your female prepared?"

"To the best of my ability." He began throwing supplies into a bag as he spoke. "But I will not take any chances with her safety. I will go to her."

"Do you need assistance?"

"No, but thank you, my friend."

Friend. How long had it been since he used that word? Morgan looked almost as startled, but he clasped his shoulder briefly before heading for the door.

"I'm going to prepare the town."

Clint was halfway to Josephine's homestead before it occurred to him that Morgan had not asked for his assistance. Apparently his... friend had understood that nothing would keep Clint away from Josephine. What of Morgan's woman, he wondered? How could he stay away from her?

Jo tossed and turned. Normally, she had no trouble sleeping thanks to the hard work she did every day, but tonight felt different. An unusual restlessness had her staring out into the night instead. Maybe a hot drink would help her relax she decided and gave up on trying to sleep.

As she sipped the tea—another one of the little luxuries Clint had provided—she tried to plan the next day's work, but it was useless. Her mind kept returning to the big cyborg. He usually showed up every third day, so she didn't expect him tomorrow and the day already seemed to stretch out interminably. It wasn't the fact that the work would be easier if he were with her, it was his actual company. Being able to look up and see his face, or to sneak a glance at that massive body, brightened her whole day.

"Some homesteader I turned out to be," she muttered. "I haven't even made it two months on my own."

As much as she had wanted her own home, her own land, sharing it with him was far more satisfying. And what if he stopped coming? How much worse would it be now that she had grown accustomed to his presence? *You can't count on him*, she tried to remind herself, but the words rang hollow. He had never yet failed to do whatever he said he would—she had no reason to think he would fail her. And yet...

Still lost in her thoughts, it took her a moment before she realized that the chickens were chirping anxiously. She frowned; they never usually stirred after dark. She glanced through one of the clear observation panels and frowned again. Was something wrong with the panel? The surrounding rock formations were dim, barely visible against the night sky—a sky where the stars had disappeared. Dust storm, she suddenly realized, her pulse increasing.

Rapidly running through her checklist, she decided she was as prepared as she could be. That knowledge only helped a little as she watched the outside visibility continue to decrease. Her heart was beating uncomfortably fast. How much she wished that Clint was here with her. His calm competence would have eased her mind considerably. And even if everything went well, these storms could last for a week or more. A week or more before she could see him again.

"You see? This is why you can't depend on anyone else. They're never around when you need them." she muttered then shook her head, knowing she was being irrational. He had no way of knowing what would happen.

The darkness increased until nothing was visible through the panels. The wind had picked up as well, and she could feel the walls of the shelter tremble. Thank goodness that she was at least partially sheltered by the ridge. Another gust shook the walls, but the shelter was well-anchored, and she remembered that Clint had gone around inspecting and strengthening every strap.

The wind roared and she huddled in the center of her mattress, all thoughts of sleep abandoned. Another gust, even louder, shook the shelter and she barely heard the outer entrance to the airlock chime. The outer door was open? Had the wind somehow breached it.? She rushed to the porthole, then breathed a sigh of relief as Clint, and Red, forced themselves inside. It was a tight fit and she waited impatiently for him to close the outer door. He moved with unusual slowness as he reached for the button, but it wasn't until the pressure equalized and she could open the inner door that she realized why.

He stumbled inside, his coat flapping oddly and to her horror she saw that it had been torn to shreds and the skin beneath it was equally shredded, blood staining much of his remaining clothing.

"Oh my god. Clint!"

She rushed to his side as he started to collapse, but he was too heavy for her to hold up. The best she could do was provide some support as he collapsed to his knees.

"Inner door," he rasped, his voice like sandpaper.

"I don't think I can get Red inside."

"Fine in airlock. Better than outside." When she still hesitated, he caught her hand. "Your safety most important."

Reluctantly, she climbed to her feet and went to the panel. The horse had not moved from his position and he seemed quite calm.

"I'm sorry," she whispered, and closed the door.

As soon as it sealed, she rushed back to Clint. Pulling out

one of her precious cleansing cloths, she dampened it with the still warm water from the kettle and began wiping gently at one of the many long gashes that covered his body. They didn't seem to be deep but there were so many of them.

"Stop," he said firmly, his voice sounding more like his usual deep tone. "They will heal."

She looked up at him and noticed for the first time that one of the lenses of his ever-present dark glasses had cracked.

"Your glasses are damaged. Why don't you take them off?"

He was shaking his head before she even finished. "No. Now listen. Did you fill the water reservoir?"

"I did yesterday."

"Top it off. If you have any spare containers fill them too."

"I have to take care of you first. You're injured."

"And I will heal. I want you to gather as much water as possible. The solar array won't be able to generate power until this passes, and the pump may shut off."

"But—"

"Water first."

"Fine." She knew he was right—it had been covered in the training manuals—but she still hated to leave his side when he was so obviously wounded.

"Josephine, look."

He held out his arm and she watched in amazement as one of the scratches closed before her eyes, leaving only a long smear of blood.

"Now go."

Forcing her eyes away from the healing process, she obeyed. By the time the reservoir was topped up, the water in the chicken habitat refreshed, and every spare container filled with water, Clint seemed to be back to his usual self. He had stripped off the damaged shirt to reveal an impressive display of hard muscle and she did her best not to stare at him as he disappeared through the airlock for a few minutes, returning with a large duffel.

"How's Red?"

"I told you he would be fine. Technically, he should actually be able to resist the full brunt of the storm but…" He shrugged, an almost uncomfortable look on his stern face. "It seemed better to provide him with what protection I could. You do not mind?"

"Of course not."

"We will need to conserve power. Is there anything else for which you will need the light?"

"We? Are you staying?"

"Josephine, I didn't ride through a dust storm just to turn around and leave."

"But why did you come?"

"This is where I want to be."

He stepped closer and her pulse raced. In the confined space, she was reminded once again of his massive size. But her pulse had not sped up due to fear. She was uncomfortably aware that her nipples had turned rock hard beneath the thin tank and her panties were growing damp. Her panties. Shit, she wasn't wearing anything else. Her cheeks heated.

"I'll just put some pants on," she said quickly, but as she bent over to retrieve them, she heard him groan.

"You do not need to cover your beauty on my account. I am used to restraining myself."

Beauty? Restraining himself? She whirled back around, holding the pants to her chest like a shield.

"What do you mean?"

"Josephine, it cannot have escaped your attention that I find you extraordinarily desirable."

"Me?" she squeaked.

"You."

He gently took her hand and placed it against the long hard ridge of his erection. Oh my. Despite her best efforts, she had noticed that he seemed to have an almost constant erection, but she had told herself that it was undoubtedly part of cyborg functionality.

"You mean you're not always like that?"

A rusty noise escaped his lips and it took her a moment to realize that it was a laugh.

"No, my little love. Just around you."

What had he said? She peeped up at him, but his face was as inscrutable as ever, perhaps more so with one of his eyes completely concealed by the cracked lens.

"Take off your glasses," she said softly.

He stiffened. "My eyes are not... human."

"Well, duh. I know that. They're better."

"Better?"

"You found the ice for me, didn't you?"

"Yes," he admitted slowly. "You will not be repulsed?"

The truth escaped before she could stop it. "Nothing about you could repulse me."

He groaned again, and then slowly, reluctantly, removed the broken glasses. She couldn't prevent the gasp that escaped, but she grabbed his arm when he immediately started to replace them.

"Don't do that. I was just surprised. They're so beautiful."

"Beautiful?" The word obviously shocked him.

"Yes," she said firmly.

It was quite true. A heavy fringe of dark lashes surrounded eyes that glowed a deep, ever-changing red. She stared, fascinated and enthralled, until he suddenly put an arm around her and pulled her up against acres of warm hard flesh. The gaps torn by the dust storm made it even easier to feel his skin against hers and she suddenly wanted to rub against him like a cat, desperate to feel all of him.

"Clint," she gasped.

"Do you know what it does to me to hear you call me by name?" he growled, grinding his erection against her. "To feel as if you see me as a man?"

"I do."

He bent over, one arm going under her butt as he lifted her until they were face to face.

"I'm not going to ask permission to kiss you," he said.

"You don't need to," she whispered, and then his mouth covered hers.

SEVEN

Josephine had seen his eyes and not rejected him. Clint's heart rejoiced as he bent his head to kiss her. She responded as eagerly as she had done the first time they kissed and this time when he slid his hand under her shirt, she didn't freeze. Watching her face carefully, he lifted the garment over her head. Small pert breasts topped with rosy pink nipples matched her slender frame, a tiny waist curving into slender but undeniably feminine hips.

"Perfect," he murmured as she blushed.

Impatient to feast his eyes on all of her, he carried her to the bed alcove and laid her across the mattress before ripping her panties away to reveal her delicate little cunt, already flushed and glistening with her desire. He shifted his vision, delighting in the heat glowing from her body with her arousal. Her hands fluttered and he knew she was fighting the urge to cover herself from his scrutiny.

"You are beautiful, Josephine. You do not need to hide from me."

"I know I'm small," she said.

"You're perfect. And look at the way you respond to me." He stroked a single finger across one tempting little nipple and felt it harden even further as she arched towards him. He continued his path down across her stomach and saw it tremble before very gently parting those delicate pink folds. Her clit was already exposed, the hood drawn back to reveal the hard little pearl. Very gently, he brushed his finger across it, and she cried out, her hips lifting. He traveled further, gliding through the slick folds to her tiny entrance. He probed very gently at the tight ring of muscle and groaned as his finger slipped inside. For the first time, he began to wonder if she would be able to take him.

"You're very tight, my love. Are you intact?"

"You mean am I a virgin?" She shook her head. "No, Nic—No."

Despite his instinctive anger at the mention of her worthless former partner, he gave a sigh of relief. Perhaps this would be possible after all.

Stroking her clit once more, he carefully added a second finger, his cock jerking as he watched her stretch to take him. She cried out, but there was no pain on her face and her hips were moving restlessly against him.

"Clint, please. I want to feel you inside me."

"Slowly," he said, to himself as much as her. "We must take it slowly."

"Yes, yes, but at least start."

He gave into temptation, ripping off his pants and notching his cock at her entrance. He pushed forward but her body resisted until he stroked across her clit again. He heard her cry out, felt the rush of heat bathe the head of his cock, and pushed again as her hips jerked towards him, her body finally accepting him into an impossibly hot, wet embrace. A streak of electricity rolled down his spine and then he was coming in helpless, shuddering waves as the endless years of loneliness finally came to an end. He had found his mate and he was never letting her go.

Jo's body hovered on the edge of climax as Clint exploded inside her. His whole body shook as he bent down over her and she put her arms around him, holding on to him with a fierce, protective tenderness. He buried his head in her neck, still shaking, and she stroked his head, even as her clit throbbed and ached.

"I'm sorry." He finally raised his head and gave her a rueful smile. "I did not expect to lose control that quickly."

"That's all right. It's actually kind of flattering. Maybe in a little while—" She broke off abruptly as she realized that even though he had come, his cock was still hard, still stretching her entrance.

"There is no need to wait. Unless you..."

"No, no. I don't want you to wait," she said immediately and tried to raise her hips, but he was so big and heavy that she had little leverage.

"I said we should take things slowly," he reminded her.

"Yes, well, you didn't take your own advice. Now it's my turn."

"Of course."

He gripped her hip with one hand and pushed deeper, his passage eased by his own fluids but still stretching her to the limit. The sensation hovered on the edge of pain but then he adjusted his angle to put pressure on her clit and the aching fullness turned into a fiery pleasure. She cried out and he covered her mouth with his, swallowing her cries as he held her in place for his thrusts, sending her ever higher until she flew over the edge, the world disintegrating into a thousand points of light as she shattered, and her climax triggered his own.

As her body finally relaxed, she realized he was wrapped around her, holding her as if she was infinitely precious. Her heart ached as she clung to him with equal intensity, the two of them together in the midst of the surrounding storm.

"You didn't ask if I was on birth control," she said curiously as Clint gently pressed a warm cloth to her still sensitive flesh. He had finally let her go so that he could tend to her. "Did you already know?"

His hand stilled for a moment before he continued. "My seed is not fertile."

"You mean you can't have children?" Her heart ached for him, and perhaps, for herself.

"No, it's still possible. But I would have to make that choice." His eyes met hers. "And I do not think that this is the time."

A sudden, unexpected longing surprised her with its intensity, but she nodded. "You're right. Mars isn't ready for children yet. There is too much work to be done."

Discarding the cloth, he climbed back into bed and settled her against him. "You are quite correct. Now you should rest."

"Yes, boss," she said, rolling her eyes, but she really was exhausted. The warmth of his body surrounded her, and she drifted off to sleep.

Despite his insistence on her need for sleep, he woke her twice more during the night to make love to her with the same passionate intensity before letting her fall back asleep.

"Are you always hard?" she murmured sleepily as he woke her for the third time, his clever fingers already teasing her clit.

"I have control over all aspects of my body," he said, then grinned at her. "Except around you."

"What does that mean?"

"I mean, my little love, that my cock does not want to respond to my orders when you're around. It is constantly hard, constantly seeking to bury itself in this tight, sweet little cunt."

He matched his actions to his words, and she arched helplessly upwards as he filled her once again. She would have sworn that her body was exhausted, but her clit was once again aching and ready.

"Of course, while I cannot seem to make it go down, I do have other ways of controlling it," he murmured.

"Like what?" she asked breathlessly, trying to lift her hips as he held her easily in place.

"Like this."

A sudden deep pulse traveled through her stretched channel, then another. Oh my god. His cock was vibrating inside her. He reached between their bodies, pressing against her clit so that the vibration traveled from her pussy to the aching nub and she came so suddenly and so hard that she was still shaking when she felt the hot rush of his seed exploding inside her.

"You are a god among men," she said seriously, and fell asleep to the sound of his laughter.

A BARELY PERCEPTIBLE LIGHTENING OF THE SKY WAS THE only sign that the next day had dawned.

"It's so dark," she said.

"The dust clouds block the sun. That's why the solar panels won't operate the water pump once we run out of whatever is stored in the batteries."

"But the RTG still works, right? We'll have heat and oxygen and the power from it."

"Yes." He smiled down at her. "Don't worry, my little love. Everything will be fine."

She believed him.

"Then I'm going to get the chores out of the way so we can relax."

"Or play some more," he suggested, cupping her breast with a big, warm hand.

"Chores first," she insisted and slipped out of bed before she gave in to the devilish look in those amazing eyes.

Despite her determination not to neglect her duties, there really wasn't much work to be done. After they tended the chickens and the garden, and performed the daily checks of the equipment, she found herself with more free time than she'd had since she landed on Mars. She would never have thought she would enjoy a week spent confined in a small space with another person, but not once did she find herself bored or annoyed. Clint occupied himself by using some of the extra materials he had brought to build a pair of chairs while she attempted to make a pot from some of the Martian regolith. They played games and experimented with the limited choice of food and inevitably wound up back in her bed.

"How did you end up in the military?" she asked once, as they lay wrapped in each other's arms.

His body went still, and she didn't think he would answer.

"I had a little sister," he said eventually. "Sweet, helpless, always full of laughter. I was working two jobs, trying to make enough money to keep us housed."

She nodded. She knew what it was like, how hard you had to work to afford even the smallest place. The only alternatives were the streets or one of the vast homeless shelters that were their own form of hell.

"But because I was gone so much, she was lonely. And because she was lonely, she let our mother back into her life. I came home one night, and she was gone. I spent a month looking for her. When I found her, she had been bought by one of those rich corporate bastards. She looked so different, more like a doll than a girl, and she didn't laugh any more. I told her I loved her; told her I would get her out of there. She said it was too late."

He gazed up at the ceiling, but she knew he was looking into the past.

"I refused to listen, of course. I went back twice, and I finally thought she was starting to listen to me. The third time I returned, the bastard was there. He told me that she had killed herself and it was my fault. He had his men beat me up and throw me out on the street. I thought I was going to die, and I didn't care."

"Oh, Clint." Tears were streaming down her face.

"It turned out that my body's will to live was stronger than my guilt," he said, his voice emotionless. "After I recovered, I joined the military. I had lost my jobs, of course, and the place where we had lived, but I didn't join because of that. In spite of everything that had happened, I hadn't completely lost my illusions. I really thought it was about helping people, that maybe I could make a difference."

"Is that why you volunteered for the cyborg program?" she asked softly.

"Volunteered? Is that what they tell you?" The sound he made could not be considered a laugh.

"You mean you didn't choose this?"

"No. If you are critically injured, they have the right to use your body in whatever way they see fit."

"Critically injured?" The thought of him dying made her heart skip a beat.

"Yes." He took her hand and placed it over his heart. "It's a new heart—the first thing they modified. Then they decided what other pieces of me they wanted to change."

"Your eyes?" she whispered.

He tried to shrug, but it was a poor effort. "They were damaged too. When they were done with me, I was no longer human."

"You are most certainly human," she said fiercely.

"Am I?" He turned to look at her, his eyes glowing in the dim light. "I don't have the same rights as a human. The same feelings."

"You feel the same to me," she said, willfully misunderstanding his words. When he opened his mouth to respond, she stopped him with a kiss. When he groaned and responded, she climbed on top of him, loving the feel of warm skin and hard muscles beneath her. Determined to make him forget about the past, at least for tonight, she slowly kissed her way down his body, lingering over the small hard nubs of his nipples until he clutched the sheet. When she reached his cock, already throbbing with desire, drops of precum pearled at the tip.

She swiped her tongue across it and they both groaned. He tasted delicious and she lapped at him eagerly, circling the swollen head and concentrating on the sensitive underside.

"Josephine!"

His hand came to her head, trying to gently pull her away, but she was determined to give him this pleasure. To give herself this pleasure, she thought as she felt him shudder when she took more of him in her mouth. Her jaw ached, stretched wide by his size, but it was worth it to feel his body tense, his hips thrusting upward, to hear him call out her name as he came in long, shuddering pulses and she drank him down.

When he finally stilled, she gave him a last slow lick, then smiled up at him, knowing he could see her even in the dim light.

"Perhaps not quite the same," she said. "But much better."

Instead of responding verbally, he reversed their positions with shocking speed.

"My turn," he growled, and she sighed happily, glad that he was no longer trapped in the past with his painful memories.

EIGHT

On the fifth day, the quiet once again woke Jo. The winds had dropped, she realized, and although a thick layer of dust covered the observation panels, she could see that the sky had lightened at last.

"I think it's over," she murmured.

"Yes," Clint agreed, and raised up on one elbow to look down at her face. "What happens now?"

"I suspect I have a lot of cleaning to do," she said lightly, despite the anxiety filling her heart. Would he feel compelled to leave now that the emergency was over? Sometime over the past week she had stopped worrying about being too dependent on him and realized that she wanted nothing more than to have him next to her.

"*We* have a lot of cleaning to do," he corrected, and her heart skipped a beat. Did that mean he wasn't leaving? "But first I need to make a circuit of my territory and ensure that no one is injured or needs assistance."

"But you'll be back?"

"Yes, my little love. And then we will talk."

Before she could respond, he dropped his head and kissed her, and she abandoned her worries to the pleasure of his touch.

When she watched him ride off, her heart ached a little, but not because she feared he would not return. She simply missed him already. Still, there was work to be done and she couldn't stand there mooning after him all day. Shaking her head, she went to start cleaning dust off the solar panels.

Later that afternoon, she was inside taking a break from the seemingly endless efforts to remove the accumulated dust. She heard the door to the airlock slide open and turned eagerly. But instead of the beloved face of her cyborg, Nicky stood there.

He looked terrible, his lean frame almost emaciated and his face gaunt, but he sauntered in as if he owned the place, removing his nose mask with a satisfied sigh.

"Nicky! What are you doing here?"

"Why did you have to choose a place so far away from town?" he complained, ignoring her question. "It took me forever to get out here."

"I don't understand. Why are you here?"

"To be with you, of course." He tried to flash her his old charming grin, but she felt nothing. The blue eyes that had once seemed so beautiful to her now looked pale and lifeless compared to the memory of Clint's ever-changing eyes. "Wasn't that our plan?"

"Until you decided you'd rather work in the power plants."

He shuddered but quickly tried to hide it, looking around the shelter instead. "I changed my mind. Gotta say you've done a great job, Josie Bear. I didn't expect you to be doing so well already." A squawk came from the greenhouse and his eyes brightened. "Is that a chicken? Why don't you make me one of our eggs for breakfast?"

As he spoke, he dropped into Clint's chair, the one he had made, looking for all the world like he expected her to wait on him.

"No, Nicky. They aren't laying yet but even if they were, they aren't your chickens and they wouldn't be your eggs."

"Don't be so selfish, Jo. This was all my idea, remember?"

"Selfish?" She could only stare at him. "Do you have any idea how hard I've worked? I'm at this from sunup to sundown and with this dust storm, we—"

She stopped abruptly but it was too late.

"We?" Any pretense of good humor slipped away. "I should have known you would find some other gullible male to take care of you."

"Some other male to take *care* of me? You never took care of me, Nicky. And I never expected that from you. All I expected was that you would keep your word and do your share."

For a moment, an expression of guilt flashed across his face, but then it hardened, and he sneered at her. "No wonder you sent me off to the power plant. You probably already had another sucker lined up."

"You were the one who chose to leave," she said quietly.

"Yeah, well, you didn't try very hard to stop me. Who's the new guy, Jo? Who's the fool who fell for those big brown eyes?"

"I am," a deep voice growled.

She had been too appalled by Nicky's complete disregard for the truth to notice the airlock door opening. Clint stood there, his eyes blazing red.

"A robot? You traded me in for a fucking robot? You little whore."

Before the words finished emerging from Nicky's mouth, Clint had his hand around his neck, lifting him easily off the floor as his fingers dug into the thin flesh. Nicky's face began to turn blue.

"No, Clint, don't. Don't hurt him." She tugged at his arm until her words finally seemed to penetrate. He dropped Nicky and stepped back, his face expressionless, but she knew him too well not to realize immediately that he had misunderstood the reason why she had stopped him.

Nicky picked himself up off the ground, the remnants of his usual swagger returning.

"See, robot? She chose me. Chose a real man."

Clint's fist clenched but he didn't move.

"No, Nicky," she said quickly. "I don't choose you. I choose Clint. I will always choose Clint."

"What?" He actually looked surprised. "But he's a goddamn machine."

"No, he isn't. He's a person—the best person I've ever met. And I love him."

Clint's eyes glowed red and he took a step towards her.

"I love you too, Josephine."

"Love?" Nicky sneered. "You don't know what the fuck love means."

"Yes, I do." Clint's eyes never left hers. "She taught me."

She smiled at him. "Maybe we taught each other."

"Oh, for fuck's sake. You two deserve each other."

"Yes, we do. Leave, Nicky. And don't come back. There is nothing for you here."

For a moment he hesitated, and she thought he would argue with her, but then his shoulders sagged in defeat. "Can you at least give me a ride—"

"No," Clint said immediately. "Leave."

Nicky's mouth opened, but then he looked at Clint and seemed to shrivel. Muttering curses under his breath, he shoved his mask back in place and disappeared through the airlock.

"Did you mean it?" Clint asked as soon as the doors closed.

"Of course, I did." Her hand reached up to cup his cheek gently. "Did you?"

"From the moment I saw you. Although it took me some time to realize what I was feeling."

He tugged her closer and she went gladly, but just as his mouth was about to descend over hers, there was a loud squeal from outside.

"What was that?"

He turned towards the door, his eyes changing color as he stared through the walls, then a broad grin spread across his face. "The worthless human just discovered that Big Red doesn't appreciate having a strange rider."

"Is Red okay?"

"He's fine." He shrugged. "The human not so much, but he's walking away."

"Good. Then we can concentrate on more important things. You really love me?"

"With everything I am."

He removed his glasses and her heart soared with happiness at the love glowing in his eyes. She nestled against him.

"I love you, too, Clint." She grinned up at him. "Does that mean you're going to stay with me from now on?"

His face sobered. "I don't want to leave you, Josephine, but this is still my territory and I will still need to patrol as well as helping out here."

"I understand." She knew how deep that vein of loyalty and concern ran. "But you'll come home to me?"

"Every night," he promised.

And looking up into those beautiful crimson eyes, she knew that he would. He would never let her down. A deep sigh escaped as she buried her head against his chest. It had taken twenty-two years and two planets, but she had finally found a home.

EPILOGUE

F*ive years later*

"Here it is! It's official—this is our land."

Josephine glowed as she waved the papers at him. They were purely symbolic, of course. What really mattered were the records in the Claims Office computers and he had hacked into those long ago to make sure that the claim was registered to her permanently. He had also purchased all of the surrounding claims in her name to make sure that they would be available when she was ready to expand, but he wasn't about to ruin her excitement by telling her.

"I knew you could do it," he said.

"That *we* could do it." For a moment her smile dimmed. "Your name should be on here too."

Amongst many other restrictions, Earth Government did not allow cyborgs to own property. Perhaps that would change in the future. Perhaps it wouldn't. What mattered right now was returning the smile to his woman's face.

"I suppose I'll just have to make sure you never want to get rid of me," he said, leaning down to nibble on the precise spot on her neck that always made her melt.

"Mmm, never." She shivered, and her small nipples peaked, but her face was still serious when she turned to face him. "You know that, right? That it's the two of us. That it will always be the two of us."

"It doesn't have to be just the two of us." He put a hand on her stomach, watching her face carefully. They had discussed this several times over the years but even though he had seen the longing in her eyes, she had refused to consider a child until they had permanent ownership of the land, until she knew for sure that their child would always have a home.

"Are you sure?" she asked.

"Yes, my little love. Are you? You know our child will never be able to return to Earth." The lower gravity of Mars meant that their child would never develop the physical strength to survive on their home planet.

"I don't consider that a loss. Earth holds no special memories for me."

"Or for me." His sister would live on in his heart, not as a part of the dirty overcrowded planet that had stolen her life.

"Then yes, please. Yes, I want to have a child with you."

With a triumphant roar, he carried her off to bed and proceeded to do his best to grant her request.

LATER THAT MORNING, JO SLIPPED OUT OF THEIR BED—A bed in an actual bedroom rather than a sleeping alcove in the wall of a shelter—leaving Clint sleeping. Although he went to bed with her each evening and seemed quite content to spend the entire night holding her in his arms, she knew he rarely actually slept. Allowing his seed to become fertile must have exhausted him, she thought with a quiet giggle. She was surprised she wasn't equally tired given his enthusiasm and his dedication to making sure she climaxed until she was limp with satisfaction. Instead, she felt surprisingly energetic.

She gave the big main room a satisfied glance as she passed through. Still sparse by Earth standards, every item in it was the result of their hard work and she loved the quiet, cozy space with the big window that looked out over their homestead and beyond. The valley was no longer completely free of habitation—more plots had been claimed on the far end and she found she didn't mind the fact that they had company. She paused a moment to admire the landscape, now softened by multiple colors of lichen and even a few specially bred alpine plants, but she had another goal in mind. She walked down the long corridor past the greenhouse that provided their food, past the long shelter that housed their growing flock of chickens, until she ended up at the small stable that separated the main buildings from the goat habitat.

Red stood at the far end, also looking out over the valley. Clint would have told her that he was only using the sunlight to recharge his batteries, but she thought there was much more to the horse than he was willing to admit. She went and stood next to the big animal, running her fingers through his mane and telling him about her plans for the future.

"What are you doing, Josephine?"

Not five minutes had passed before she heard the deep voice behind her. She laughed as she looked over her shoulder. "I thought you were sleeping."

"How can I sleep when my beautiful wife is not beside me?"

"I'm sorry. I didn't mean to disturb you. I just came to tell Red."

"Tell him what?"

"That this is our home now. Our permanent home." She gave Red one last pat on his metal neck and walked over to her husband. Their marriage was not official, of course—another benefit denied to cyborgs—but the ties between them were every bit as binding as those approved by the government.

"Our home," he echoed as he watched her walk towards him.

His eyes swirled and she knew he was running through his various types of vision. He had confessed to her that he found it comforting to be able to see her no matter what. His expression suddenly changed, and he dropped to his knees in front of her.

"Clint! What is it? What's wrong?"

"Nothing." A broad smile split his face as he looked up at her. "You're pregnant."

"What? How can you possibly tell already? It's been less than an hour."

"I can see my nanites." He placed a big hand across her womb. "They're glowing."

"Really?" Tears started streaming down her cheeks and she knelt in front of him. "We're going to have a baby?"

"Yes." His crimson eyes glowed with happiness. "I love you, Josephine."

"I love you, too."

And he cradled her and their child as they looked out over their valley, over their new home on Mars, the planet where their dreams had come true.

AUTHOR'S NOTE

Thank you so much for reading **High Plains Cyborg**! I hope you enjoyed reading it as much as I enjoyed writing it! This series allows me to combine my love of cyborgs and Westerns and science fiction and, of course, Mars! I've been fascinated by Mars since I first read Edgar Rice Burroughs and his tales of Barsoom. Although I don't have thoats and bejeweled princesses, my version of Mars is also fictionalized. While many of the things I touch on in the story have a scientific basis, I have taken some liberties with what is possible, at least currently.

Whether you enjoyed the story or not, it would mean the world to me if you left an honest review on Amazon. Reviews are one of the best ways to reach other readers!

I have the best readers and I appreciate you all so much! I also have to give a special thank you to Janet S. for a fast and thoughtful beta read.

So what's next on Mars? As you might imagine, M-231 is ready for a woman of his own!

AUTHOR'S NOTE

In ***The Good, the Bad, and the Cyborg***, a desperate widow needs a helping hand… and a cybernetic one might be just be perfect for the job!

Available for pre-order now on Amazon.com!

And if you'd like to keep up with all the latest developments on Mars, or any of my other series, please visit my website at www.honeyphillips.com!

ALSO BY HONEY PHILLIPS

The Alien Invasion Series
Alien Selection
Alien Conquest
Alien Prisoner
Alien Breeder
Alien Alliance
Alien Hope

The Alien Abduction Series
Anna and the Alien
Beth and the Barbarian
Cam and the Conqueror
Deb and the Demon
Ella and the Emperor
Faith and the Fighter
Greta and the Gargoyle

Cosmic Fairy Tales
Jackie and the Giant

Treasured by the Alien
with Bex McLynn
Mama and the Alien Warrior
A Son for the Alien Warrior

Printed in Great Britain
by Amazon